Grover Takes Care of Baby

By Emily Thompson

Illustrated by Tom Cooke

This educational book was created in cooperation with the Children's Television Workshop, producers of Sesame Street. Children do not have to watch the television show to benefit from this book. Workshop revenues from this product will be used to help CTW educational projects.

A SESAME STREET/GOLDEN PRESS BOOK

Published by Western Publishing Company, Inc., in conjunction with Children's Television Workshop.

While walking home from the playground one day Grover dropped his ball, and it rolled right under a baby carriage.

"Please excuse me," said Grover. "Oh, hello, Marsha! Who is this?"

"Hi, Grover," said Marsha. "This is Max, my baby brother. I'm taking care of him while Mommy and Daddy are at work."

"Oh, he is cute and adorable!" said Grover. "What do you do with him?"

"I play with him, take him for walks, help feed him, give him his baths, and put him to bed," said Marsha.

"I would like to take care of a baby, too," said Grover. "I have a new baby cousin named Emily. I, lovable, helpful old Grover, would take good care of the baby Emily."

Grover waved good-bye to Marsha and Max.

I would let her play with my toys.

I would show Emily how to climb mountains...

go through tunnels...

and leap tall buildings in a single bound!

If Baby Emily came for a visit, she could take a nap in my zoo.

I would help her get dressed.

I would introduce Emily to all my friends at play group. Oh, I would be so proud!

But what if she tore my picture? Oh, I would be so embarrassed!

Mrs. Brown would say, "Never mind, Grover, we can fix it."

After play group, we could go shopping…

and for a walk.

We could do our exercises together. One and two and—pant, pant!—three. Now touch those toes!

We could play peekaboo...

and eensy-weensy spider.

At dinnertime I would help my mommy feed
Emily in her high chair. I would tie on her bib, and
make sure her milk wasn't too hot, and cut up her
carrots, and wipe up her dribbles.

"Emily, sweetie, you need a bath. You are a mess!"

At bathtime I would be ready.

I would pour in the bubbles...

and test the temperature.

Then I would duck.

At bedtime I would help Emily listen to a story.

Then I would sing her a lullaby, kiss her nose, and turn on the night-light. I would even let her borrow my teddy monster to cuddle.

"Good night, Baby Emily."

"I, Grover, would be a big help," he said proudly.

"Oh, Grover, I am so glad you are home," said Grover's mommy as she opened the door of their apartment. "Guess what! Aunt Betsy and Uncle Ralph are bringing your baby cousin, Emily, for a visit. How would you like to help take care of the baby?"

"Grover, you are very good at taking care of baby monster!" said his mommy.